PERRO GRANDE...
PERRO PEQUEÑO

BIG DOG... LITTLE DOG

A Random House PICTUREBACK®

P. D. Eastman

PERRO GRANDE...
BIG DOG...

un cuento de las buenas noches
A Bedtime Story

Spanish translation Copyright © 1982 by Random House, Inc. Copyright © 1973 by P. D. Eastman. All rights reserved under International and Pan-American Copyright Conventions. Published in the United States by Random House, Inc., New York, and simultaneously in Canada by Random House of Canada Limited, Toronto.
Library of Congress Cataloging in Publication Data:
Eastman, P.D. (Philip D.) Perro grande . . . perro pequeño = Big dog . . . little dog. Translation of: Big dog . . . little dog. SUMMARY: Two dogs are opposite in every way, but are the very best of friends. [1. Dogs—Fiction. 2. Friendship—Fiction] I. Title. PZ7.E1314Bi 1982 [E] 81-12070 ISBN: 0-394-85142-0 (pbk.); 0-394-95142-5 (lib. bdg.) AACR2
Manufactured in the United States of America 40 39 38 37 36

PERRO PEQUEÑO
LITTLE DOG

translated into Spanish by Pilar de Cuenca and Inés Alvarez

Random House New York

Fred y Ted eran amigos.

Fred and Ted were friends.

Fred era grande.

Fred was big.

Ted era pequeño.

Ted was little.

Fred siempre tenía dinero.

Fred always had money.

Ted nunca tenía un centavo.

Ted was always broke.

Cuando caminaban bajo la lluvia, Fred se mojaba pero Ted quedaba seco.

When they walked in the rain, Fred got wet but Ted stayed dry.

A los dos les gustaba la música.
Fred tocaba la flauta.

They both liked music.
Fred played the flute.

Ted tocaba la tuba.

Ted played the tuba.

Cuando cenaban, Fred comía espinaca . . .
y Ted comía remolacha.

When they had dinner, Fred ate the spinach . . .
and Ted ate the beets.

Cuando pintaban la casa, Ted usaba pintura roja.
Fred usaba pintura verde.

When they painted the house, Ted used red paint.
Fred used green.

Un día Fred y Ted fueron de viaje.

One day Fred and Ted took a trip.

Fred iba en su automóvil verde.

Fred went in his green car.

Ted iba en su automóvil rojo.

Ted went in his red car.

Fred manejaba su automóvil despacio.

Fred drove his car slowly.

Ted manejaba su automóvil deprisa.

Ted drove his car fast.

Cuando llegaron a las montañas,
Ted esquió el día entero.

When they got to the mountains,
Ted skied all day long.

Fred patinó el día entero.

Fred skated all day long.

Al anochecer ambos estaban muy cansados.
"¡Mira!" dijo Fred. "¡Un hotelito!"

By nighttime both of them were very tired.
"Look!" said Fred. "A small hotel!"

Fred tomó un cuarto
en los altos.

Fred got a
room upstairs.

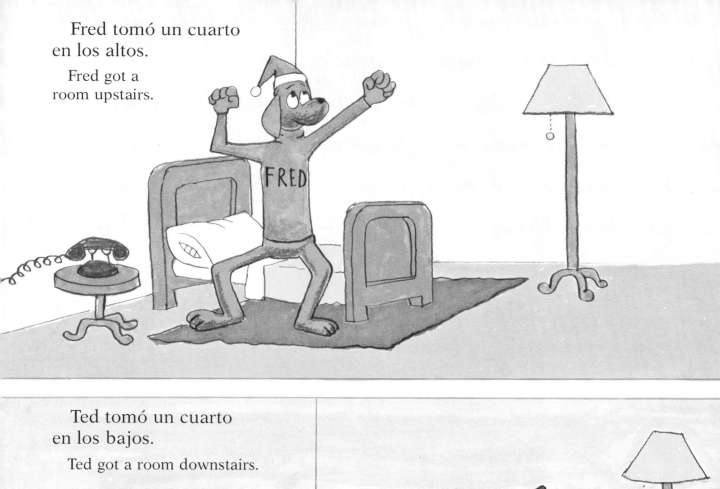

Ted tomó un cuarto
en los bajos.

Ted got a room downstairs.

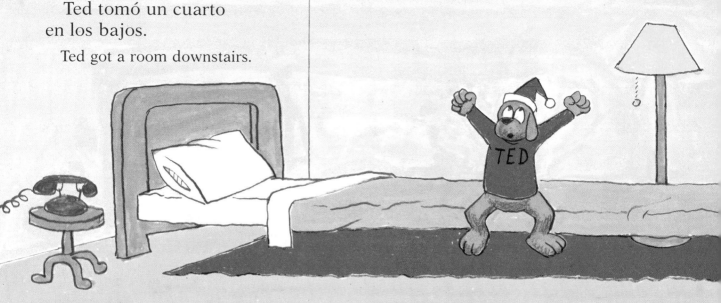

"Buenas noches, Ted.
Que duermas bien," dijo Fred.

"Good night, Ted.
Sleep well," said Fred.

"Buenas noches, Fred.
Que duermas bien," dijo Ted.

"Good night, Fred.
Sleep well," said Ted.

Pero *no* durmieron bien. Arriba, Fred daba porrazos y trompazos y se meneaba y volteaba.

But they did *not* sleep well. Upstairs, Fred thumped and bumped and tossed and turned.

Y abajo, Ted gemía y gruñía y rechinaba y se agitaba por toda la cama.

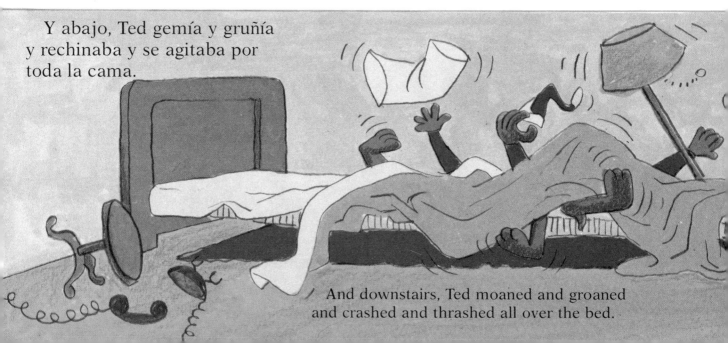

And downstairs, Ted moaned and groaned and crashed and thrashed all over the bed.

Al amanecer Fred llamó por teléfono.
When morning came, Fred called on the phone.

"Vamos a pasear,"
dijo Fred a Ted.

"Let's take a walk,"
Fred said to Ted.

"¡Qué buena idea!" dijo Ted a Fred.
"Podemos pasear y conversar."

"A good idea!" said Ted to Fred.
"We can walk and talk."

Caminaron cuesta arriba.

They walked uphill.

Caminaron cuesta abajo.

They walked downhill.

Hablaron de cosas importantes.

They made tall talk.

Hablaron de cosas
sin importancia.

They made small talk.

"¿Pudiste dormir anoche, Ted?"

"Did you get any sleep
last night, Ted?"

"¡Ni un pestañazo, Fred!"

"Not a wink, Fred!"

"¡Mi cama es muy pequeña!"

"My bed is too little!"

"¡Mi cama es muy grande!"

"My bed is too big!"

"¿Qué podemos hacer, Ted?"
"No sé, Fred."

"What can we do about it, Ted?"
"I don't know, Fred."

"¡Sé lo que hay que hacer!" dijo el pájaro. "Sólo cambien de cuartos. ¡Ted debe dormir en los altos y Fred debe dormir en los bajos!"

"I know what to do!" said the bird. "Just switch rooms. Ted should sleep upstairs and Fred should sleep downstairs!"

"¡Seguro!"

"Of course!"

"El pájaro dio en el clavo."

"The bird's got the word."

"¡A la cama!" gritó Ted.

"Back to bed!" yelled Ted.

"¡A la cama!" gritó Fred.

"Back to bed!" yelled Fred.

"Yo voy abajo," gritó Fred.
"Yo voy arriba," gritó Ted.

"It's downstairs for me," yelled Fred.
"It's upstairs for me," yelled Ted.

Ted saltó a la camita en los altos.

Ted jumped into the little bed upstairs.

Y Fred saltó a la cama grande en los bajos.

And Fred jumped into the big bed downstairs.

Ted durmió todo el día en la camita cómoda.

Ted slept all day long in the cozy little bed.

Y Fred durmió todo el día en la cama grande cómoda.

And Fred slept all day in the cozy big bed.

"Bueno, eso fue fácil de resolver.
Los perros grandes necesitan camas grandes.
Los perros pequeños necesitan camas pequeñas.
   "¿Por qué buscar problemas donde no los hay?"

"Well, that was easy to fix. Big dogs need
big beds. Little dogs need little beds.
   "Why make big problems out of little problems?"